For my brother, Pete.

First published in Great Britain in 2022 by Andersen Press Ltd.,
20 Vauxhall Bridge Road, London, SW1V 2SA, UK • Vijverlaan 48, 3062 HL Rotterdam, Nederland
Copyright © Robert Starling 2022. The right of Robert Starling to be identified as the author and illustrator of this work
has been asserted by him in accordance with the Copyright, Designs and Patents Act, 1988.
All rights reserved. Printed and bound in China.
1 3 5 7 9 10 8 6 4 2
British Library Cataloguing in Publication Data available. ISBN 978 1 78344 915 6

MIX
Paper from
responsible sources
FSC
www.fsc.org
FSC® C104723

ROBERT STARLING

Newcastle
City Council

Newcastle Libraries and Information Service

☎ **0191 277 4100**

Ⓐ

ANDERSEN PRESS

This is Fergal.

He's a very
friendly chap,

but sometimes...

Fergal tells fibs.

Like when he found three coins.

"Wow," said Beaver, "is that your money Fergal?"

"Yes," fibbed Fergal. "Let's buy some sweets."

Or when he knocked over the milk.

On Sunday morning, Fergal set off for football practice. On the way he did a really big kick... and broke Bear's bakery window.

"Fergal, did you see who broke my window?" asked Bear.
"No," fibbed Fergal.

On the football field Fergal was playing with his friends when the coach stopped the game.

"Someone has broken the bakery window. Does anyone know something about this?" asked Coach.

"No," said Fergal's friends.
"No," fibbed Fergal.

The next day, Fox wasn't at football practice. "Fox isn't coming to football," Fergal overheard Coach say, "because he broke the window and didn't tell the truth."

Fergal felt terrible for the whole afternoon.
"Are you OK, Fergal?" asked Beaver.
"I'm fine," fibbed Fergal.

At dinner Fergal's tummy felt funny.
It didn't seem to want any food.
"Fergal, do you feel poorly?"
asked his dad.

"I'M FINE!"
shouted Fergal.

On Friday, Fergal and Beaver met
Fox in the park. Fox looked so
sad about the football.
"I didn't do it," said Fox. "Honest."

The feeling in Fergal's tummy got bigger.

It was like carrying a heavy weight around.

At football on Sunday Fergal really did feel sick.
He had to sit out the game.

He waited until everyone else went home, and then tugged the coach's arm. "Coach... it was... me who broke the window."

Coach was really angry – Fergal had lied and let Fox take the blame. Owning up was only the first step in making things right.

To make up for breaking his window, Fergal helped Bear in the shop every day.

Coach decided Fergal wasn't allowed to play football for the rest of the summer.

Dear Fox,
I'm REALLY sorry I got you in trouble and didn't say it was me. You are amazing at football. I am bad at being a friend. So sorry and hope you feel better soon.
Love,
Fergal

But that had given him lots of time to work out
a way to say his most important sorry.

Fergal still likes to make things up. But now he tells everyone when he is going to do it.

And that turns fibs into stories.